The Comp
Vo

MW00987810

The Prisoner
of the
Caucasus

Leo Tolstoy

NEWCOMB LIVRARIA
PRESS

Contents

There was a baron serving as an officer in the Caucasus. His name was Zhilin.

One day he received a letter from home. His old mother wrote to him: "I am old now, and I want to see my favorite son before I die. Come to say goodbye to me, bury him, and then, with God, go back to service. And I've found you a bride: she's smart and good, and I have an estate. You may fall in love with her, and you'll marry and stay.

Zhilin thought: "Indeed, the old woman has become bad, maybe I won't have to see her. And if the bride is good, we may marry."

He went to the colonel, got a leave of absence, bade farewell to his comrades, gave his soldiers four buckets of vodka as a farewell, and got ready to go.

There was war in the Caucasus at that time. The roads were not passable day or night. If any of the Russians left or moved away from the fortress, the Tatars would either kill them or take them to the mountains. And it was established that twice a week from fortress to fortress went escorting soldiers. In front and behind went the soldiers, and in the middle rode the people.

It was summer. The wagons gathered at dawn for the fortress, the escorting soldiers came out and rode along the road. Zhilin rode on horseback, and his cart with his belongings was in the wagon.

The journey was twenty-five miles. The cart was going quietly: then the soldiers stopped, then someone's wheel or horse got loose in the cart, and everyone stood waiting.

The sun had already passed midday, and the wagon had only passed half of the road. Dust, heat, the sun was burning, and there was nowhere to take shelter. The steppe was bare: not a tree or a bush on the road.

Zhilin rode forward, stopped and waited for the wagon to approach him. He hears a horn playing behind him, so he stood still again. Zhilin thought: "Shouldn't I leave alone, without soldiers? I have a good horse under me, and if I attack the Tartars, I'll ride away. Or not to ride?..."

He stopped, thinking. And another officer Kostylin, with a rifle, rides up to him on horseback and says:

- "Let's go, Zhilin, alone. I'm exhausted, I'm hungry, and it's hot. You can't even wring out my shirt. - And Kostylin is a heavy, fat man, all red and sweat is pouring off him. Zhilin thought about it and said:

- Is the gun loaded?

- Loaded.

- Well, let's go. But we have an agreement not to split up.

And they drove ahead on the road. They rode along the steppe, talking and looking around. They could see far away.

When the steppe ended, the road entered a gorge between two mountains. Zhilin says:

- "We must go to the mountain to look, or here, perhaps, they will jump out of the mountain, and you won't see.

And Kostylin said:

- What is there to see? Let's go forward.

Zhilin didn't listen to him.

- "No," he said, "you wait below, and I'll just have a look.

And let the horse go to the left, up the mountain. The horse under Zhilin was a hunter's horse (he had paid a hundred roubles for it as a foal in the herd and had ridden it himself); it carried him up the hill as if on wings. He just jumped out - look, and in front of him, on a tithe of space, there were Tartars on horseback. A man thirty. He saw it, began to turn back; and the Tatars saw it, started to go to it, themselves on a gallop take out guns from covers. Zhilin ran under the circle with all his horse's legs, shouting to Kostylin:

- "Take out your gun! - And he thought to his horse: "Mother, take it out, don't get your foot caught; if you stumble, you're lost. When I get to the gun, I will not give myself up."

But Kostylin, instead of waiting, just when he saw the Tartars, rolled as fast as he could to the fortress. He roasted his horse with a whip from one side and from the other. Only in the dust one can see the horse's tail twirling.

Zhilin sees it's no good. The rifle is gone, nothing can be done with one saber. He let the horse go back to the soldiers - he thought to leave. He sees six men riding in front of him. The horse under him was good, and under those even kinder, and they were riding in front of him. He started to turn back, he wanted to turn back, but the horse was blown away - he couldn't hold it, he was flying straight at them. He saw a Tatar on a gray horse with a red beard coming towards him. He shrieked, his teeth bared, his rifle at the ready.

"Well," thinks Zhilin, "I know you devils: if they take me alive, they'll put me in a pit and flog me. I won't give you alive..."

But Zhilin, though not big in stature, was good at it. He took out his saber, let his horse go straight at the red Tatar, thinking: "Either I'll crush him with my horse, or I'll cut him down with my saber.

Zhilin did not get to the horse - they shot him from behind with rifles and hit the horse. The horse hit the ground with all its might and fell on Zhilin's leg.

He wanted to get up, but two stinking Tartars were sitting on him, twisting his arms back. He rushed up, threw off the Tartars, and three of them jumped down from their horses and began to beat him on the head with rifle butts. His eyes blurred and he staggered. The Tartars seized him, took off the saddles, twisted his hands behind his back, tied them in a Tatar knot and dragged him to the saddle. They knocked off his hat, pulled off his boots, searched everything - money and watches were taken out, his dress was torn. Zhilin looked back at his horse. She, the hearty one, had fallen on her side and was still lying there, but she was kicking her legs - she couldn't reach the ground; there was a hole in her head, and black blood was whistling from the hole - the dust was wet with dust for an arshin. One Tatar came to the horse, began to take off the saddle, - it was still beating; he took out a dagger and cut its throat. The horse whistled from its throat, trembled - and steamed away.

The Tartars took off the saddle and harness. A Tatar with a red beard sat on a horse, and others put Zhilin on his saddle, and in order not to fall down, they pulled him by his belt to the Tatar and took him to the mountains.

Zhilin sits behind the Tatar, swaying, poking his face into the stinking Tatar's back. All he sees in front of him is a big Tatar back, and a wiry neck, and a shaved back of his head, which is blue from under his cap. Zhilin's head was shattered, the blood caked over his eyes. And he can neither get better on horseback nor wipe the blood off. His arms were so twisted that his collarbone was broken.

They rode for a long time up the mountain, crossed the ford of the river, got on the road and rode along the gully.

Zhilin wanted to mark the road where they were taking him, but his eyes were smeared with blood, and he could not turn around.

It began to get dusk: we crossed another river, began to climb a stone mountain, smelled smoke, and the dogs barked. We came to aul. Tartars got off their horses, Tatar boys gathered, surrounded Zhilin, squeaking, rejoicing, began to shoot stones at him.

The Tatar drove the boys away, took Zhilin off his horse and called a worker. A Nogai came, a skinny man, wearing only a shirt. His shirt was ragged, his chest was bare. The Tatar ordered something to him. The worker brought a block: two oak logs on iron rings, and in one ring there was a punch and a lock.

They untied Zhilin's hands, put on the block and led him to the barn; they pushed him in and locked the door. Zhilin fell on the dung. He lay down, groped in the dark where it was softer, and lay down.

II

Almost all that night Zhilin did not sleep. The nights were short. He saw a glow in the crevice. So Zhilin got up, dug a bigger hole and began to look.

He could see the road going uphill, a Tatar sakla to the right, two trees near it. A black dog lies on the threshold, a goat and goats are walking - twitching their tails. He sees a young Tatar woman coming from under the mountain, wearing a colored shirt, pants and boots, her head covered with a caftan, and a large tin jug of water on her head. She walks, her back shakes, bends over, and by the hand she leads a shaven-headed Tatar in a single shirt. The Tatar woman went into the hut with water, and out came the Tatar of yesterday with a red beard, wearing a silk beshmet, a silver dagger on his belt, and barefoot shoes. On his head he wore a tall, black sheep's cap, folded back. He came out, stretching, stroking his red beard. He stood there, said something to the worker and went somewhere.

Then two boys rode by on horses to the watering hole. The horses were snorting wet. Some more shaven-headed boys ran out in their shirts, without socks, gathered in a bunch, came to the barn, took a twig and stuck it in the crack. As if Zhilin would duck at them: the boys squealed, ran away - only their bare knees glistened.

And Zhilin was thirsty, his throat was dry. He thinks: "I wish they'd come to check on him". He hears them unlocking the barn. A red Tatar came, and with him another, smaller in stature, blackish. His eyes are black, light-colored, ruddy, his beard is small and trimmed; his face is cheerful, he laughs all the time. The blackish one was dressed even better: a blue silk beshamet, lined with galunts. The dagger on his belt is big, silver; his shoes are red, morocco, also lined with silver. And on the thin clogs are other thick clogs. A tall white lamb's hat.

The red Tatar came in, said something, as if cursing, and stood leaning on the doorpost, wiggling his dagger, like a wolf squinting at Zhilin. And the black-haired one, quick and lively, so all on springs and walking, came straight to Zhilin, squatted down, grinned, touched him on the shoulder, began to murmur something in his own way, winking his eyes, clicking his tongue. He keeps saying:

- "Korosho Urus! Korosho Urus!

Zhilin didn't understand anything and said:

- Give me some water to drink.

The black one laughs.

- "Korosho urus," he mumbles in his own way.

Zhilin showed with his lips and hands that he should drink.

The black man understood, laughed, looked out the door and called someone:

- "Dina!

A girl came running, thin, slim, about thirteen years old, with a face like the black man's. You could see that she was his daughter. Her eyes were black, light-colored and her face was beautiful. She was wearing a long blue shirt with wide sleeves and no belt. On the floors, on the chest and on the sleeves is trimmed with red. On her feet are pants and slippers, and on the slippers others, with high heels, on her neck a monisto, all of Russian fifty pieces. Her head was uncovered, her braid was black, and in her braid was a ribbon, and on the ribbon were plaques and a silver ruble.

Her father told her to do something. She ran away and came back again, bringing a tin jug. She gave her water and squatted down, all bent so that her shoulders went below her knees. She sat there, her eyes open, looking at Zhilin as he drank - as at some beast.

Zhilin gave her back the jug. She jumped away like a wild goat. Even her father laughed. He sent her somewhere else. She took the jug, ran, brought some unleavened bread on a round board and sat down again, bent over, keeping her eyes open, watching.

The Tartars left, locked the doors again. A little while later a Nogay came to Zhilin and said:

- "Ayda, master, ayda!

He doesn't know Russian either. Zhilin only realized that he was telling him to go somewhere.

Zhilin went with the block, he limped, could not step, and turned his leg to the side. Zhilin followed the Nogai. He saw a Tatar village, ten houses and their church with a turret. By one house there are three horses in saddles. Boys are leading them. A black-haired Tatar jumped out of the house and waved his hand for Zhilin to come to him. He laughs, says something in his own way, and went out the door. Zhilin came to the house. The living room was good, the walls were smoothly smeared with clay. In the front wall there were colorful down jackets, and on the sides there were expensive carpets; on the carpets there were guns, pistols, a checkers - all in silver. In one wall there was a small stove flush with the floor. The floor is earthen, clean as a current, and the whole front corner is covered with felts; there are carpets on the felts, and down cushions on the carpets. And on the carpets there are Tartars sitting in their clogs: a black man, a red man and three guests. They have down cushions behind their backs, and in front of them on a round board there are millet pancakes, and cow's butter in a cup, and Tatar beer - buza - in a jug. They eat with their hands, and their hands are all covered with oil.

The black man jumped up, ordered to put Zhilin to the side, not on the carpet, but on the bare floor; he climbed up on the carpet again, treating the guests with pancakes and bouza. The worker put Zhilin in his place, took off his top shoes, put them in a row by the door, where other shoes stood, and sat down on the felt closer to the hosts, watching them eat, wiping his drool.

When the Tartars had eaten the pancakes, a Tatar woman came, wearing a shirt like the girl and pants; her head was covered with a scarf. She took away butter and pancakes, gave a good bowl and a jug with a narrow sock. The Tartars began to wash their hands, then folded their hands, sat on their knees, blew in all directions and recited prayers. They talked in their own way. Then one of the Tatar guests turned to Zhilin and began to speak Russian.

- Kazi-Mughamet took you," he said, pointing to the red Tatar, "and gave you to Abdul-Murat," pointing to the blackish one. Abdul-Murat is your master now.

Zhilin is silent. Abdul-Murat started to speak and kept pointing at Zhilin, laughing and saying:

- "Soldier, Urus, Korosho, Urus.

The interpreter said:

- He tells you to write a letter home, so that they will send a ransom for you. As soon as they send the money, he will let you go.

Zhilin thought about it and said:

- "How much ransom does he want?

The Tartars talked, and the interpreter said:

- Three thousand coins.

- No," said Zhilin, "I cannot pay that.

Abdul jumped up, started waving his hands, saying something to Zhilin, thinking that he would understand. The interpreter translated and said:

- How much will you give?

Zhilin thought about it and said:

- Five hundred rubles.

Then the Tatars began to talk a lot, all of a sudden. Abdul began to shout at the red one, and started to whisper so much that drool spurted from his mouth.

But the red one only squinted and clicked his tongue.

They fell silent, the interpreter spoke:

- "Five hundred rubles isn't enough for the master's ransom. He paid 200 rubles for you himself. Kazi-Mughamet owed him. He took you for a debt. Three thousand rubles, you can't let him pay less. If you don't write, they'll put you in a pit and punish you with a lash.

"Eh," thought Zhilin, "it's worse to be timid with them.

He jumped to his feet and said:

- And you tell him, the dog, that if he wants to frighten me, I will not give him a penny, nor will I write to him. I was not afraid of you dogs, and I will not be afraid of you.

The interpreter retold the story, and suddenly they all started talking again.

The black man jumped up and approached Zhilin.

- Urus, - he said, - dzhigit, dzhigit Urus!

Dzhigit means "good man" in their language. And he himself laughs; he says something to the interpreter, and the interpreter says:

- "Give me a thousand rubles.

Zhilin stood his ground:

- "I won't give you more than 500 rubles. And if you kill him, you won't get anything.

The Tatars talked and sent a worker somewhere, while they looked at Zhilin and at the door. When the worker came, a tall, fat, barefooted and shabby man followed him; he also had a shoe on his foot.

And Zhilin gasped - he recognized Kostylin. And they caught him. They sat them down side by side; they began to tell each other, and the Tartars were silent, watching.

Zhilin told them how it had happened to him; Kostylin told them that the horse under him had gotten under him and his rifle had malfunctioned, and that Abdul had caught up with him and taken him.

Abdul jumped up, pointed at Kostylin and said something. The interpreter translated that they were both of the same master now, and that whoever gave money first would be released first.

- Here," he said to Zhilin, "you are still angry, but your comrade is calm; he has written a letter home, five thousand coins will be sent. He will be well fed and not offended.

So Zhilin said:

- "The comrade is as he wills, he may be rich, but I am not. I'll do as I say," he says. If you want, kill him, it won't do you any good, but I won't write more than 500 rubles.

They were silent. Suddenly Abdul jumped up, took out a trunk, took out a quill, a scrap of paper and ink, gave it to Zhilin, clapped him on the shoulder, and said: "Write." He agreed to five hundred rubles.

- Wait a moment," said Zhilin to the interpreter, "tell him to feed us well, clothe and clothe us properly, and keep us together, so that we may have more fun, and to take off the shoe.

He looks at his master and laughs. The master laughs too. He listens and says:

- "I'll give you the best clothes: a Circassian coat and boots, even if you want to get married. I'll feed them like princes. And if they want to live together, let them live in a barn. You can't take off the shoe, they'll leave. I'll only take it off at night. - He jumped up and patted me on the shoulder. - Yours is good, mine is good!

Zhilin wrote a letter, but wrote it wrong on the letter, so that it wouldn't get through. He thought to himself: "I'll leave."

They took Zhilin and Kostylin to a barn, brought them corn straw, water in a jug, bread, two old coats and ragged soldier's boots. They must have taken them from the dead soldiers. For the night they took off their stocks and locked them in the barn.

III

Zhilin and his comrade lived like that for a month. The master kept laughing: "Yours, Ivan, is good, and mine, Abdul, is good". But he fed him badly - all he gave him was unleavened bread made of millet flour, baked flatbread, or even unbaked dough.

Kostylin wrote home once more, still waiting for the money to be sent, and was bored. All day long he sat in the barn, counting the days until the letter came, or sleeping. But Zhilin knew that his letter would not reach him, and he did not write another.

"Where," he thought, "would my mother get so much money to pay for me? And she lived the more that I sent her. If I were to raise five hundred roubles for her, I should be ruined; God willing, I shall get out of it myself."

And he kept looking around, asking how he could escape.

He walks about the aul, whistling; sometimes he sits and makes handicrafts, or sculpts dolls out of clay, or weaves wicker from twigs. And Zhilin was a master of every kind of handicraft.

Once he made a doll with a nose, arms, legs and a Tatar shirt, and put the doll on the roof.

The Tatar women went to fetch water. The owner's daughter Dinka saw the doll and called the Tatar girls.

They put the jugs together, looking at it, laughing. Zhilin took off the doll and gave it to them. They laugh, but dare not take it. He left the doll, went into the barn and watched what would happen?

Dina ran up, looked back, grabbed the doll and ran away.

The next morning, Dina came to the doorstep at dawn with the doll. And the doll was covered with red rags and rocked like a child, rocking herself in her own way. The old woman came out, scolded her, snatched the doll, broke it, and sent Dina off to work somewhere.

Zhilin made another doll, even better, and gave it to Dina. Once Dina brought a jug, set it down, sat down and looked at it, laughing herself, pointing at the jug.

"Why is she happy?" - thought Zhilin. He took the jug and started to drink. He thought it was water, but there was milk. He drank the milk.

- "Good," he says.

How happy Dina is!

- Good, Ivan, good! - and she jumped up, clapped her hands, snatched the jug and ran away.

And from then on she began to bring him milk every day. And when the Tartars made cheese cakes from goat's milk and dried them on the roofs, she secretly brought them to him. And once the master was cutting a ram, so she brought him a piece of mutton in a sleeve. She would drop it and run away.

There was once a heavy thunderstorm, and it rained like a bucket for an hour. And all the rivers became muddy. Where there was a ford, there was three inches of water and the rocks were tumbling. Streams flowed everywhere, and the mountains rumbled. When the thunderstorm passed, streams were running everywhere in the village. Zhilin asked his master for a knife, cut out a roller and planks, made a wheel, and attached dolls to the wheel at both ends.

The girls brought him some rags, and he dressed the dolls: one was a man, the other a woman; he approved them and put the wheel on the brook. The wheel spun, and the dolls jumped.

The whole village gathered: boys, girls, women; and the Tatars came, clicking their tongues:

- Ay, Urus! Ivan!

Abdul had a broken Russian watch. He called Zhilin, showed it to him, clicking his tongue. Zhilin said:

- Let me fix it.

He took it, took it apart with a knife, put it apart, made it good again and gave it to him. The clock works.

The owner was glad, brought him his old, ragged beshmet and gave it to him. He took it: it was good enough to cover himself at night.

From that time Zhilin was known to be a master. People started to come to him from distant villages: some of them would bring him a lock for a gun or a pistol, some of them would bring a watch. His master brought him some tools: pliers, tweezers, boraxes, and a file.

Once a Tatar fell ill, they came to Zhilin: "Come and cure him. Zhilin doesn't know how to treat him. He went and looked at him, thinking: "Maybe he'll get well on his own". He went to the barn, took water and sand, stirred it up. In front of the Tartars he whispered on the water and gave it to him to drink. The Tatar recovered to his luck. Zhilin began to understand a little in their language. And those Tartars got used to him, when necessary, they called him "Ivan, Ivan"; and those who still squinted at him as if he were a beast.

The Red Tatar did not like Zhilin. As soon as he saw him, he would frown and turn away, or curse him. There was also an old man. He did not live in the village, but came from under the mountain. Zhilin saw him only when he went to the mosque to pray to God. He was small in stature, with a white towel wrapped around his hat. His beard and mustache were trimmed, white as down; but his face was wrinkled and red like a brick; his nose was hooked like a hawk's, and his eyes were gray, evil, and he had no teeth, only two fangs. He would walk in his turban, propped up on a crutch, looking around like a wolf. When he sees Zhilin, he snores and turns away.

Once Zhilin went under the mountain to see where the old man lived. He went down the path and saw a garden, a stone fence, cherry trees, whispering trees and a hut with a flat lid. When he came closer, he saw beehives made of straw, and bees were flying and buzzing. And the old man was on his knees, doing something at the hive. Zhilin climbed up to look higher and rattled the block. The old man looked back and squealed, grabbed a pistol from his belt and shot Zhilin. He had only just managed to duck behind a rock.

The old man came to his master to complain. The master called Zhilin, laughing and asking him:

- "Why did you go to the old man?

- I did him no harm," he said. I wanted to see how he lived.

The master gave it to him. And the old man was angry, hissing, whispering something, showing his fangs, waving his hands at Zhilin.

Zhilin didn't understand everything, but he realized that the old man was telling his master to kill the Russians, not to keep them in the village. The old man left.

Zhilin began to ask the master: who is this old man? The master said:

- This is a big man! He was the first dzhigit, he beat many Russians, he was rich. He had three wives and eight sons.

They all lived in the same village. The Russians came, ruined the village and killed seven sons. One son remained and was passed on to the Russians. The old man went and passed on to the Russians himself. He stayed with them for three months; he found his son there, killed him himself and fled. Since then he gave up fighting and went to Mecca to pray to God, from which he has a turban. Whoever has been to Mecca is called a haji and wears a turban. He does not love your brother. He tells me to kill you; but I can't kill you, I paid money for you; but I love you, Ivan; I wouldn't even let you go if I hadn't given you a word. - Laughing, he said in Russian: "Yours, Ivan, is good - mine, Abdul, is good!

IV

Zhilin lived like that for a month. During the day he walks around the aul or does handicrafts, and when night comes, it gets quiet in the aul, so he digs in his shed. It was difficult to dig from stones, but he rubbed stones with a file, and he dug a hole under the wall, that it was enough to crawl through. "Only if only," he thought, "I would know the place well, in which direction to go. But no one tells the Tartars."

So he chose the time when the master left; he went in the afternoon behind the aul, on the mountain - he wanted to see the place from there. And when the master was leaving, he ordered the little one to follow Zhilin, not to let him out of his sight. The little one ran after Zhilin, shouting:

- "Don't go! His father didn't tell him to. I'll call the people!

Zhilin started to persuade him.

- I will not go far," he said, "I will only go up that mountain, I need to find herbs to cure your people. Come with me; I won't run away with the stake. And tomorrow I'll make you a bow and arrows.

I've persuaded the boy, let's go. It's not far to look at the mountain, but it's hard to climb with the stake. Zhilin sat down and began to look at the place. At noon [At noon - to the south, at sunrise - to the east, at sunset - to the west] behind the barn there was a hollow, a herd was walking, and another aul in a low spot could be seen. From the aul there is another mountain, even steeper; and behind that mountain there is another mountain. Between the mountains there is a blue forest, and there are more mountains, rising higher and higher. And above them all the mountains are white as sugar under the snow. And one snow mountain is higher than the others with a cap. At sunrise and sunset the mountains are the same, and somewhere auls are smoking in the gorges. "Well," he thought, "this is their side.

He began to look at the Russian side: there was a river under his feet, an aul of his own, gardens all around. On the river - like small dolls, you can see - women sit, rinsing. Behind the aul there is a lower mountain and through it two more mountains, there is a forest along them; and between the two mountains there is a flat place, and on the flat place far away there is smoke. Zhilin began to remember when he lived at home in the fortress, where the sun rose and where it set. He saw that there, in that valley, must be our fortress. There, between these two mountains, we must run to it.

The sun began to set. The snowy mountains turned scarlet from white; the black mountains turned dark; steam rose from the ravines, and the very valley where our fortress should be, was on fire from the sunset.

Zhilin began to gaze - something was looming in the valley, like smoke from chimneys. And he thought that it was the Russian fortress.

It was getting late. I heard the mullah shout. The herd is being driven - the cows are roaring. The little one keeps calling: "Let's go", but Zhilin doesn't want to leave.

So they returned home. "Well," thought Zhilin, "now I know the place, I must run away. He wanted to run away that very night. The nights were dark, - the damage of the month. By evening the Tartars returned. They used to come and bring cattle with them and come cheerful. But this time they brought nothing and brought their murdered Tatar, the red-haired brother, on a saddle. They came angry and gathered to bury him. Zhilin came out to watch. They wrapped the dead man in a cloth, without a coffin, carried him under the chenar trees outside the village, laid him on the grass. The mullah came, the old men gathered, tied their hats with towels, took off their shoes, sat down in a row on their heels in front of the dead man.

The mullah was in front, three old men in turbans were sitting in a row behind them, and there were more Tartars behind them. They sat down, stooped and kept silent. They were silent for a long time. The mullah raised his head and said:

- Allah! (means God.) - He said this one word, and again they shut their mouths and remained silent for a long time; they sat without moving.

Again the mullah raised his head:

- "Allah!" and they all said: "Allah" and again fell silent. A dead man lying on the grass did not move, and they were sitting as dead. Not one of them moves. Only they could hear the leaves on the chinar tree turning in the breeze. Then the mullah read a prayer, everybody got up, lifted the dead man in their arms and carried him. They brought him to the pit; the pit was not a simple one, but dug under the ground, like a cellar. They took the dead man under the arms and under the skirts, bent him over, lowered him down a little, put him under the ground, tucked his hands on his belly.

The Nogay brought green reeds, they laid a hole with reeds, filled it with earth, leveled it, and put a stone in the dead man's head. They trampled the earth and sat down in a row in front of the grave. They were silent for a long time.

- Alla! Alla! Alla! - They sighed and stood up.

The red-haired man handed out money to the old men, then stood up, took a whip, struck himself three times on the forehead and went home.

The next morning Zhilin saw the red mare leading the red one out of the village, and three Tartars following him. When they came out of the village, the red man took off his beshmet, rolled up his sleeves - he had big arms - took out his dagger and sharpened it on a bar. The Tartars pulled the mare's head upwards, the red-haired man came up, cut the throat, threw the mare down and began to skin it, tearing the skin with his fists. The women and girls came and began to wash the guts and gut. Then they cut up the mare and dragged her into the hut. And the whole village gathered at the redhead's house to remember the dead man.

For three days they ate the mare, drank booze - they remembered the dead man. All the Tatars were at home. On the fourth day, Zhilin saw them going somewhere at lunchtime. They brought horses, cleaned up, and ten men went, and the red one went; only Abdul stayed at home. The month was just emerging - the nights were still dark.

"Well," thought Zhilin, "we must run away now," and he said to Kostylin. And Kostylin was frightened.

- How can we run, we don't even know the way.

- I know the way.

- And we won't get there at night.

- And if we don't make it, we'll stop in the woods. I've got some flatbread. Why are you going to sit here? It's good if they send money, or they won't even collect it. And the

Tatars are angry now, because the Russians killed their son. They say they want to kill us.

Kostylin thought about it.

- Well, let's go!

V

Zhilin went into the hole, dug it wide enough for Kostylin to get through, and they sat waiting for the aul to be quiet.

When the people in the village quieted down, Zhilin climbed under the wall and got out. He whispered to Kostylin:

- "Get in.

Kostylin climbed up, but caught a stone with his foot, and it rattled. And the master had a guard - a colorful dog. And a wicked, angry dog; its name was Ulyashin. Zhilin had already fed it in advance. When Ulyashin heard him, he shrieked and rushed off, followed by the other dogs. Zhilin whistled a little, threw a piece of flatbread - Ulyashin recognized it, waved his tail and stopped yapping.

The master heard, and barked from the hut:

- "Gait! Gait, Ulyashin!

And Zhilin scratched Ulyashin behind the ears. The dog was silent, rubbing against his legs, wagging his tail.

They sat around the corner. Everything quieted down, only they could hear a sheep farting in the hut and water rustling on the stones below. It was dark, the stars were high in the sky; the young moon was reddened above the mountain, and it was coming up with horns. In the ravines the fog is as white as milk.

Zhilin got up and said to his comrade:

- "Well, brother, let's go!

They set off, and just as they moved away, they heard the mullah on the roof singing: "Alla, Besmilla! Ilrahman!" So the people will go to the mosque. Oli again, hiding under the wall.

They sat for a long time, waiting for the people to pass. It got quiet again.

- Well, with God! - They crossed themselves and went. They went across the courtyard to the river, crossed the river, went through the gully. The fog was thick, but the stars were visible above their heads. Zhilin notes by the stars which way to go. It was fresh in the fog, it was easy to walk, but his boots were awkward and stubborn. Zhilin took off his boots, threw them on and walked barefoot. He bounces from pebble to pebble and looks at the stars. Kostylin began to lag behind.

- "Hush," he said, "go on; the damned boots have wiped off all your feet.

- Take them off, it'll be easier.

Kostylin went barefoot - even worse: he cut all his feet on the stones and kept lagging behind. Zhilin said to him:

- "Your feet will heal, but if they catch up with you, they'll kill you, worse.

Kostylin said nothing, walking, grunting. They walked downhill for a long time. They heard dogs yelping to the right. Zhilin stopped, looked around, climbed up the mountain, felt with his hands.

- Eh," he said, "we made a mistake - we went to the right. There's a foreign aul here, I saw it from the mountain; we must go back and to the left, up the mountain. There must be a forest here.

And Kostylin says:

- "Wait just a little, let me breathe, my feet are all bloody.

- Hey, brother, they'll heal; you jump lighter. That's how it is!

And Zhilin ran back and to the left up the mountain, into the forest.

Kostylin kept lagging behind and sighing. Zhilin shouts and shouts at him, but he keeps going.

They climbed up the mountain. That's right - a forest. We entered the forest, we tore off the last of our dress on the thorns. They attacked a path in the forest. They're coming.

- Stop! - A hoof stamped on the road. They stopped and listened. It stamped like a horse and stopped. When they moved off, it stopped again. When they stop, it will stop. Zhilin crawled up and looked at the light on the road - there was something standing there: a horse was not a horse, and something strange on the horse, something that did not look like a man. It snorted - he hears it. "What a miracle!" Zhilin whistled softly, and as it shuffled off the road into the forest, it rattled through the forest, as if a storm were flying, breaking the limbs.

Kostylin fell with fear. And Zhilin laughs and says:

- It's a deer. Hear the horns breaking the forest. We're afraid of him, and he's afraid of us.

Let's go on. Already the Vysozhars have started to descend, it won't be long before morning. But whether they are going there or not, they don't know. So Zhilin thinks that this is the road they took him on, and that it will be ten miles to his own, but there is no sure sign, and you can't tell at night. When they came to a clearing, Kostylin sat down and said:

- "As you wish, but I will not go: my legs are not going.

Zhilin began to persuade him.

- "No," he said, "I can't walk, I can't.

Zhilin got angry, spat and cursed him.

- So I'll go alone, goodbye.

Kostylin jumped up and set off. They walked about four versts. The fog in the forest was even thicker, they could see nothing in front of them, and the stars were barely visible.

Suddenly they heard a horse stomping ahead. They could hear it clinging to the rocks with its horseshoes. Zhilin lay down on his belly and listened to the ground.

- That's right, a horse is coming this way!

They ran off the road, sat down in the bushes and waited. Zhilin crawled up to the road and looked - a Tatar on horseback was coming, driving a cow. He was purring something to himself. The Tatar passed by. Zhilin returned to Kostylin.

- Well, God has passed by; get up, let's go.

Kostylin started to get up and fell down.

- I can't, by God, I can't, I can't, I'm exhausted.

He was a heavy, plump man, sweating, and as the cold fog enveloped him in the forest, and his legs were peeled off, he became stiff. Zhilin began to lift him by force. Kostylin screamed:

- "Oh, it hurts!

Zhilin froze.

- Why are you shouting? The Tatar is close by, he'll hear. - And he thought to himself: "He's really relaxed, what shall I do with him? It's not good to abandon a comrade."

- Well," he said, "get up, sit on my stakes, I'll carry him, if you can't walk.

He put Kostylin on himself, took his hands under his thighs, went out on the road and dragged him.

- Only," he said, "don't crush me by the throat with your hands for Christ's sake. Hold on to my shoulders.

It's hard for Zhilin, his legs are bloody and he's exhausted. He bends over, adjusts his legs, throws him up so that Kostylin could sit higher on him, and drags him along the road.

The Tatar must have heard Kostylin shouting. Zhilin hears someone coming from behind, calling in his own way. Zhilin rushed into the bushes. The Tatar took out his rifle, fired a shot, failed, squealed in his own way and galloped away along the road.

- Well," said Zhilin, "we're lost, brother! He, the dog, is about to gather the Tartars after us in pursuit. If we don't go three versts away, we're lost. - And he thought to

Kostylin: "And I was damned to take this deck with me. I would have left long ago on my own."

Kostylin said:

- "Go alone, why should you be lost because of me?

- No, I won't go: it's not right to leave a comrade behind.

So he took me on his shoulders again and started off. He went on like that for about a mile. Still the forest was coming, and he couldn't see the way out. And the fog began to clear, and as if the clouds began to come in. He couldn't see the stars. Zhilin was exhausted.

He came to a spring by the roadside, lined with stones. He stopped, took Kostylin down.

- "Let me rest," he said, "I'll have a drink. We'll eat some flatbread. It must be not far

As soon as he lay down to drink, he heard a footstep behind him. They rushed to the right again, into the bushes, under the bush, and lay down.

They heard Tatar voices; the Tatars stopped at the very place where they had turned off the road. They talked, and then they barked, as dogs are trained. They heard something crackling in the bushes, and someone else's dog came straight to them. It stopped and barked.

The Tartars, too, are strangers; they grabbed them, put them on horses and took them away.

They traveled three versts, and Abdul the owner met them with two Tatars. He said something to the Tatars, they put them on their horses and took them back to the village.

Abdul did not laugh and did not speak a word to them.

They brought him to the aul at dawn and put him in the street. The boys came running. They beat them with stones and whips, squealing.

The Tatars gathered in a circle, and an old man from under the mountain came. They began to talk. Zhilin hears that they are judging about them, what to do with them.

Some say they should send them further into the mountains, but the old man says:

- We should kill them.

Abdul argues and says:

- I gave money for them. I'll ransom them.

And the old man says:

- They won't pay anything, they'll only cause trouble. And it's a sin to feed the Russians. Kill them and it's over.

We parted. The master came to Zhilin and began to say to him.

- If," he said, "they don't send me a ransom for you, I'll have you dead in two weeks. And if you try to run away again, I'll kill you like a dog. Write a letter, write it well.

They brought them papers, they wrote letters. They put stocks on them and took them behind the mosque. There was a hole five arshins high, and they lowered them into the hole.

VI

Their life became very bad. They did not take off the stocks and did not let them out into the open. They threw unbaked dough there, like dogs, and drained water in a jug. Stench in the pit, stuffiness, wetness. Kostylin became sick, swollen, and his whole body was aching, and he moaned or slept. And Zhilin is gloomy, he sees it's bad. And he didn't know how to get out.

He started to dig, but there was nowhere to throw the earth, the owner saw him and threatened to kill him.

Once he was squatting in the pit, thinking about his free life, and he was bored. Suddenly, a flatbread fell on his knees, and another, and cherries sprinkled. He looked up and there was Dina. She looked at him, laughed and ran away. Zhilin thought: "Won't Dina help?"

He cleared a place in the hole, dug up some clay and began to mold dolls. He made people, horses, dogs; he thought: "When Dina comes, I'll throw them to her".

Only the next day Dina was gone. And Zhilin hears horses clattering, some drove by, and the Tatars gathered at the mosque, arguing, shouting and reminiscing about the Russians. And he hears the voice of an old man. He could not make out well, and guesses that the Russians came close, and the Tatars were afraid, as if they had not entered the village, and did not know what to do with the prisoners.

They talked and left. Suddenly he hears something rustling upstairs. He saw Dina squatting on her knees, her knees above her head, hanging down, monists hanging, dangling above the pit. Her eyes were shining like stars. I took two cheese cakes out of my sleeve and threw them to him. Zhilin took them and said:

- "How long has it been since you've been here? I made you some toys. Here, here! - He started throwing her one at a time, but she shook her head and didn't look.

- Don't! - She said. She sat for a while and said: Ivan, they want to kill you. - She puts her hand on her neck.

- Who wants to kill me?

- My father, the old men tell him to, but I feel sorry for you.

So Zhilin says:

- "If you feel sorry for me, bring me a long stick.

She shakes her head, saying she can't. He folds his hands and prays to her.

- Dina, please. Dina, bring it to me.

- "You can't," she said, "they'll see, everyone's home. - And she left.

So Zhilin sits in the evening and thinks: "What will happen?" He keeps looking up. The stars are visible, but the month hasn't risen yet. The mullah shouted, everything went quiet. Zhilin began to doze off, thinking: "The wench will be afraid".

Suddenly clay fell on his head, he looked up and saw a long pole poking at the edge of the pit. He poked, started to descend, and crawled into the pit. Zhilin rejoiced, grabbed it with his hand and pulled it down; it was a big pole. He had seen this pole on the master's roof before.

He looked up: the stars were shining high in the sky, and above the pit, like a cat's, Dina's eyes were glowing in the dark. She bent down with her face on the edge of the pit and whispered:

- "Ivan, Ivan!" And she kept waving her hands in front of her face, saying, "Quiet, please.

- What? - says Zhilin.

- They've all left, only two of them are home.

Zhilin says:

- "Well, Kostylin, let's go and try one last time. I'll give you a seat.

Kostylin doesn't want to hear it.

- No," says he, "I can't go out of here. Where shall I go when I can't even turn around?

- Well, so farewell, don't let it go to waste. - I kissed Kostylin.

I grabbed the pole, told Dina to hold it and climbed up. He broke off twice, the block was in the way. Kostylin supported him and he climbed up. Dina was pulling his shirt with her hands as hard as she could, laughing herself. He took Zhilin's pole and said:

- "Take it down, Dina, or they'll grab it and kill you. - She dragged the pole, and Zhilin went under the mountain. He climbed down under the hill, took a sharp stone and began to unscrew the lock. But the lock was strong, he couldn't break it, and it was awkward. He heard someone running down the mountain, jumping lightly. He thought: "That's right, it's Dina again." Dina came running, took a stone and said:

- "Let me.

She sat down on her knees and began to turn it out. But her hands were as thin as twigs, she had no strength. She dropped the stone and cried. Zhilin began to pick the lock again, and Dina squatted beside him, holding him by the shoulder. Zhilin looked back and saw a red glow behind the mountain to the left. The month is rising. "Well, he thought, - before the month we must go through the gully and get to the forest." He got up, threw a stone. Even in a shoe, but we must go.

- Goodbye," he said, "Dinushka. I'll remember you forever.

Dina clung to him, fumbling with her hands, looking for a place to put the flatbread. He took the flatbread.

- "Thank you," he said, "good girl. Who will make dolls for you without me? And he stroked her head.

Dina cried, covered herself with her hands and ran up the mountain like a goat. Only in the darkness she could hear the monsters in her braid rattling on her back.

Zhilin crossed himself, picked up the lock on the shoe with his hand so that it wouldn't rattle, and walked along the road, dragging his feet, while he kept looking at the dawn, where the month was rising. He recognized the road. It was eight miles straight ahead. He would only have to reach the forest before the month came out. He crossed the river: the light behind the mountain had already turned white. He went down the gully, walking along, looking at himself: he could not see the month yet. The dawn has already lightened up and on one side of the gully it is getting lighter and lighter. A shadow is creeping under the mountain, coming closer and closer to him.

Zhilin is walking, still keeping to the shadow. He is in a hurry, but the month is getting out even sooner; even to the right the tops of the trees are lit up. When he began to approach the forest, the month came out from behind the mountains - it was white and bright, just like daytime. All the leaves on the trees were visible. It was quiet and light in the mountains: it was as if everything had died out. Only you can hear the river murmuring below.

When he reached the forest, no one caught him. Zhilin chose a darker place in the forest and sat down to rest.

He rested, ate a flatbread. He found a stone and started to break the block again. He beat all his hands, but didn't knock it down. He got up and walked down the road. He walked about a mile, exhausted and his legs were breaking. He steps ten steps and stops. "There's nothing to do," he thought, "I'll drag on as long as I have strength. And if I sit down, I will never get up. I will not reach the fortress, but as soon as it dawns, I will lie down in the forest, in the front, and at night I will go again.

All night long he walked. Only two Tartars on horseback came across, but Zhilin heard them from afar and hid behind a tree.

The month began to pale, the dew fell, close to the light, and Zhilin did not reach the edge of the forest. "Well," he thought, "I will walk thirty paces more, turn into the forest and sit down. He walked thirty steps and saw that the forest was ending. He came to the edge - it was quite light; as on the palm of his hand there was a steppe and a fortress in front of him, and to the left, close under the mountain, fires were burning, extinguishing, smoke was drifting, and people were at the fires.

He took a closer look and saw: guns shining - Cossacks, soldiers.

Zhilin rejoiced, gathered his last strength and went up the mountain. And he thought: "God forbid that a Tatar on horseback would see him here, in a clear field: even if it was close, you wouldn't get away".

Just when he thought about it, he saw three Tartars standing on a hillock to the left, two tithes. When they saw him, they rushed towards him. That's how his heart broke. He waved his hands and shouted with all his might to his men:

- "Brothers! Help me! Brothers!

Our people heard. The Cossacks on horseback jumped out and rushed towards him - in front of the Tatars.

The Cossacks are far away, but the Tartars are close. And Zhilin gathered himself with the last strength, picked up the block with his hand, ran to the Cossacks, but he couldn't remember himself, crossing himself and shouting:

- "Brothers! Brothers! Brothers! Brothers!

There were fifteen Cossacks.

The Tartars were frightened and began to stop before they reached the road. And Zhilin ran up to the Cossacks.

The Cossacks surrounded him and asked him: who was he, what kind of man was he, where did he come from? And Zhilin couldn't remember himself, crying and saying:

- "Brothers! Brothers!

Soldiers ran out, surrounded Zhilin - some of them gave him bread, some porridge, some vodka; some of them covered him with overcoats, and some of them broke the block.

The officers recognized him and took him to the fortress. The soldiers rejoiced, their comrades gathered to see Zhilin.

Zhilin told them how it was with him and said:

- "I've gone home and got married! No, I guess it wasn't my destiny.

And he stayed to serve in the Caucasus. And Kostylin was bought back a month later for 5,000. He was barely alive when they brought him back.

Afterword by the Translator

The Luminary of Moscow: Tolstoy's Metapolitics and Oceanic Telos of Mankind

Tolstoy stands among the minds of the late 19th century as one of the greatest anti-Ideologues of his century His literature remains some of the greatest storytelling ever written- deeply spiritual, philosophic and prophetic. Prophetic in his prediction that the Socialist policies of the revolutionaries would end in great horrors, spiritual in his deep Oceanic wonder that is woven throughout his art- a wonder trying to find a certainty of knowledge- and philosophic in his intellectual meditations which are simultaneously individualistic but Synergistic, cosmic in scope but filled with intimate psychological portraiture. A depth of compassion for all living souls pervades his works. His hate was mostly vectored towards that which should be hated- war, injustice and oppression of the poor, which his pen pal Gandhi founded his movement upon. Tolstoy was insistent on his belief that no government, socio-political ideology or movement could fix society. Rather, the individual's spiritual and moral development was the only hope for society- a belief that led him to reject Socialism and criticize the Russian Czarist state. His work oscillates between the immanence of individual experience and personal moral responsibility, and the cosmic interconnectivity of all humans throughout all time- a reflection of Schopenhauer's collective unconscious.

Tolstoy left an unmanageable corpus behind. He produced hundreds of novels, novellas, short stories and fables, didactic guides, academic briefs, poetry collections, political and geopolitical theorems, religious catechisms and constantly published articles on issues of the day. Tolstoy's earliest novels, such as the trilogy "Childhood" (1852) and "Boyhood" (1854) and Youth (1857), were largely autobiographical in nature. They were deeply romantic in nature, reflecting the Franco-German Romantic themes personified by writers like Goethe, Schiller and Rousseau, whom Tolstoy read. They had a focus on individual experience rather than broader social and philosophical themes. His early diaries, however, show a constant preoccupation with broader moral issues. In the middle of his career, Tolstoy became oceanic in focus, a shift that was in part caused by his reading of Continental philosophy. His historical fiction was interwoven with social issues and spiritual contemporary and produced his magnum opus, "War and Peace" (1869). While it retained his acute psychological insights into individual experience, it also explored profound philosophical questions about the nature of war, history, and human agency. Tolstoy employed a vast canvas, intertwining the personal stories of his characters with the grand sweep of historical events, demonstrating his ability to capture the intricacies of human existence within the tapestry of society. Following the publication of his greatest novels, Tolstoy entered a period of spiritual and philosophical introspection that profoundly influenced his subsequent works. This phase is characterized by his exploration of moral dilemmas, the nature of faith, and the pursuit of a meaningful life. Works like "Anna Karenina" (1877) and "The Death of Ivan Ilyich" (1886) delve into the complexities of societal expectations, and the existential challenges of confronting mortality. This emphasis on death pervades all of his works from there on out.

In his later years, Tolstoy became an even deeper Stoic, finally rejecting his place of privilege (he was born into a rich family) and underwent a deeper spiritual awakening that led him to question his own privileged position in society and to embrace a life of simplicity and moral rigor. He gave away his possessions and titles, and lived an ascetic life. This marked a significant shift in his writing, as he increasingly focused on themes related to social injustice, poverty, and the quest for a more egalitarian society. He began as a sceptic, but became a philosopher-ascetic. His works during this period, including "Resurrection" (1899) and "The Kingdom of God Is Within You" (1894), reflect his deepening engagement with issues of social reform and nonviolent resistance. He wrote some of his most poignant philosophic works during this period. In his final years of life, he lived as an ascetic and focused entirely on philosophical and religious treatises, where he delineated his radical ideas on nonviolence, pacifism, and the rejection of wealth and power. These works, such as "What Is Art?" (1897) and "Confession" (1882), showcase his attempts to reconcile his spiritual beliefs with the realities of the world. They are lofty and oceanic, which meant they were interpreted in many different directions. The Communist regime which took power only a few years after his death utilized his words to justify their totalitarianism, but later banned Tolstoy and Dostoevsky due to their spiritual themes and emphasis on individual morality.

Continental Connections: The Epic Telos of Mankind

The darker strains of Tolstoy's thought, which would eventually get him Excommunicated from the church, comes at least in part from the Pessimistic, Subjectivist and sometimes Nihilistic philosophy of Schopenhauer and Schopenhauer's apprentice, Nietzsche. Tolstoy taught himself German (his wife was German) and French fluently. Tolstoy read Schopenhauer's massive work of Platonic Atheism "The World as Will and Representation," and was captivated by his expansive analysis of human desires, suffering, and the illusory nature of the world. Schopenhauer's emphasis on the insatiable nature of human desires and the resultant dissatisfaction struck a chord with Tolstoy's own observations of the human experience. Tolstoy's engagement with Schopenhauer's ideas is evident in his later works, where he explores themes of disillusionment, existential despair, and the transient nature of human happiness. Tolstoy acknowledged Nietzsche's influence, stating in a October 10, 1893 diary entry, "Nietzsche has a mind for the exceptional...in him, as in none other, is felt a profounder knowledge of what a human being is." In his novella "The Death of Ivan Ilyich," Tolstoy grapples with the futility of worldly pursuits and the inevitability of death, themes that bear a resemblance to Schopenhauer's pessimistic outlook that would eventually be picked up by Kafka. However, he certainly was not a Pessimist all the way through, and contradicted both Nietzsche and Schopenhauer on several fundamental points. Nietzsche advocated for a full renunciation of all moral values, taking it further than Schopenhauer by rejecting the Genealogy of Morals entirely. For Tolstoy, this was an evil and self-destructive path, and the true answer lay in a return to moral values, love, and the pursuit of a life of simplicity and authenticity. Nietzsche and Tolstoy would have despised each other if they had ever met. But this oceanic vision of his own philosophy where Tolstoy quite literally tried to fix all of the fundamental problems of humanity in one go is very much reminiscent of his reading of Continental idealism via Hegel, Schopenhauer and Nietzsche, who asserted vast metaphysical systems aimed at understanding all of reality. This scope of his philosophic project Tolstoy lifted from the German Philosophers of the 19th and early 20th century.

Nietzsche likewise ready Tolstoy and a bit of Dostoevsky before he died, mentioning Tolstoy briefly in his Genealogy of Morals with a dismissive note:

For nothing!", "Nada!" - nothing thrives and grows here, at most Petersburgers Metapolitics and Tolstoyan "pity"

Tolstoy and Dostoevsky: The Twin Metaphysicians of St. Petersburg and Moscow

The mirror metaphysicians were contemporaries. Tolstoy mentioned Dostoevsky in his diary from November 16, 1869, "Dostoevsky is the only psychologist from whom I have something to learn; he is truly great and his works are precious to me." Dostoevsky in a letter to his brother dated November 1, 1880 wrote, "I think that when it comes to depicting real, everyday life, Tolstoy is unrivalled. No one can match him." Fyodor Dostoevsky hailed Tolstoy as a genius, and vice versa, but expressed reservations about the practicality of his philosophy. Both Dostoevsky and Tolstoy shared a deep concern for moral dilemmas facing Russia on the precipice of a violent revolution and the existential struggles of humanity. Both writers were Stoics- asserting that the individual must take responsibility not just for their own sins, but their capacity for sin, and without belief in the divine there is no hope for humanity. Dostoevsky was much more practical than Tolstoy, who often asserted a utopian vision for humanity with only a simple piety as the path towards this utopia.

Tolstoy and Dostoevsky were both convinced of the inevitability of Religion. While the "demons" from central European Materialism were convincing the Russian intelligentsia that presuppositionless rationality was progress, both Tolstoy and Dostoevsky saw this as self-deception. For the allegedly pure rationalism of the Post-Protestant world was driven by metaphysical principles, rendering these new "progressive ideas" insidiously and darkly religious in nature. Even Freud, who himself argued for presuppositionless science, called Marxism "Darkly Hegelian" and "Suspiciously Metaphysical". For Socialism's tenants are based in a Telos- a moral value hierarchy which decides on what the ideal society looks like. It's an Eschatology of sorts that claims to be beyond religion, but is itself a religion. Tolstoy writes:

It is impossible for there to be a person with no religion (i.e. without any kind of relationship to the world) as it is for there to be a person without a heart. He may not know that he has a religion, just as a person may not know that he has a heart, but it is no more possible for a person to exist without a religion than without a heart.

Still, Tolstoy was in constant conflict with coherent religious ideologies. This peaked with his excommunication from the Orthodox church just a few years before his death, after decades of arguments with the church. This did not bother him, as he had been questioning and attacking the doctrines of the church, and writes at the beginning of his Confession:

I was baptized and brought up in the Orthodox Christian faith. I was taught it both from childhood and throughout my adolescence and youth. But when I left the second year of university at the age of 18, I no longer believed in anything I had been taught.

In Resurrection, he mocks the "church Christians" who turn to the spiritual writers instead of the "real" intellectuals like his beloved Schopenhauer:

And so, to clarify this question, he took not Voltaire, Schopenhauer, Spencer, Comte, but the philosophical books of Hegel and the religious works of Vinet, Khomyakov, and, naturally, found in them just what he needed: a semblance of soothing and justification of the religious teaching in which he was brought up and which his mind had long since allowed, but without which all life was filled with troubles, and in recognizing which all these troubles were immediately eliminated.

You can see how Tolstoy was halfway between Orthodox Epistemology and the new Central European Protestant ideologies of Subjectivity and Perspectivism under the new religion Modernism. Tolstoy rejected the idea that one can be religionless, but adopted the Protestant anti-metaphysical belief that one can be "traditionless" and subsequently that one can be somehow magically Christian but not a part of the institution Christ Himself founded. He critiqued organized religious institutions not from a place of presuppositionless rationality, but from a religious institution composed of one: Tolstoy's church. Tolstoy developed a cult following, ironically creating a para-church hierarchy of authority. This is also one of the central problems that George Orwell points out about Marxism, most famously in Animal Farm- that hierarchies are inevitable, not optional. And if you destroy "institutional" Christianity, you are not actually destroying hierarchies, but rather creating new, hidden and insidious hierarchies of power. So when Protestants abandoned the institution of the church, just like

Socialism supposedly abandoned the oppressive hierarchy of "Capitalism", this was little more than self-deception, because all that was happening was the replacement of a clear, obvious and responsible hierarchy with a hidden, pernicious and unaccountable hierarchy. A shadow hierarchy that cannot be fixed or held responsible. A relationship with a transcendent always binds one to the others in that same pattern of worship, as Kierkegaard writes "only in relationship with the Other am I free", so Tolstoy's belief in worship apart from, or outside of, the institution of the church is self-deception. Tolstoy adopted this central European fallacy, exactly how Dostoevsky describes it in Demons. The philosophic disease of Luther' nascent Sola Scriptura Atheism (the Geneva ideas as Dostoevsky referred to them as) impacted Tolstoy and the rest of the Russian Intelligentsia exactly like a parasite, making the violence, genocides and radical socio-political ideologies of the October Revolution inevitable. Tolstoy's deviation into Subjective spirituality and Protestant-style self-deception follows the exact path Dostoevsky sketches out in Demons.

Once one believes that being a "traditionless" or "institutionless" Christian is possible, that the church is merely a category of people with similar presuppositional beliefs, not an Apostolic institution, Atheism and the breakdown of Atheism into Deconstructivist Post-Modernism is inevitable. As soon as one believes that "God has no representatives on earth", or Christianity is "a relationship not a religion", subjectivity has been instantiated as the fundamental Epistemological model, the Logos has been replaced with a flat rationalism as the core animating nature of reality. The self-deceptive belief that one is following "the bible not tradition" is Metaphysical Subjectivity masquerading as Absolutism. There is a very short distance between a Protestant stating, "I stand upon the Word of God alone" and "there are an infinite number of Genders". Sola Scriptura always leads to reality-collapse as it renders faith a merely axiomatic rationalism predicated upon a personal subjective interpretation of truth. Reality is now a Subjective Experience (me reading my Bible by myself and determining truth), not a super-rational objective and unchanging revelation that is knowable through relationship and inevitably manifest as a spiritual institution, as Orthodoxy holds. In other words, the path of Self-Deception looks like the following:

Traditionlessness [Protestantism / Individualism] >
Religionlessness [Atheism/ flat rationalism] >
Realitylessness [Modernism & Post-Modernism]

In Tolstoy, we see these central European "Idols" (Solzhenitsyn) or "Demons" (Dostoevsky) of Post-Protestant Subjectivity poisoning his otherwise profound Epistemological musings. Schopenhauer notes this inevitably of irreligion from Protestantism in The World as Will and Representation:

> The essence of Protestantism is individualism, which necessarily leads to subjectivism, and this, in turn, to the denial of objective truth.. Protestantism, by rejecting celibacy and actual asceticism in general [i.e. replacement of Stoicism with Epicureanism], as well as its representatives, the saints, has become a blunted, or rather broken-off Christianity, lacking the pinnacle: it runs out into nothing.... by eliminating asceticism and its central point, the merit of celibacy, has actually already abandoned the innermost core of Christianity and is to that extent to be regarded as apostasy from it. This has become evident in our days in the gradual transition of Christianity into the flat rationalism, this modern Pelagianism...

This "gradual transition" of Christianity into the "flat rationalism" of secularism which Schopenhauer observed in his day is now a universal law; there has never been a Protestant society that has not secularized. There are only Catholic and Orthodox countries left in the world, and "bible believing" non-denominationalism is the fastest shrinking religion on earth, for wherever it spreads, a deep and permanent Atheism is only 2-3 generations behind.

Tolstoy walked the edge between this Pessimistic

Subjectivity derived from Protestantism and the faith of his youth. In his later works "What is My Faith?" and "The Study of Dogmatic Theology" he explicitly affirms the Christian faith, but also critiques dogmatic theology and advocates for a more individual and personal interpretation of faith, a subjectivism he received from Schopenhauer's Post-Protestant Rationalism. Still, Tolstoy keeps this Subjectivism largely tethered to Theism, unlike Schopenhauer. Toward the end of Confessions, he writes about this return to a child-like faith:

> And I turned to the study of the very theology which I had once so contemptuously cast aside as unnecessary...That there is truth in the doctrine is certain to me; but it is also certain that there is falsehood in it, and I must find the truth and the falsehood and separate the one from the other. And so I set about it. What I have found false in this doctrine, what I have found true, and what conclusions I have arrived at, constitute the following parts of the essay, which, if it is worthwhile and needed by anyone, will probably be printed sometime and somewhere.

Dostoevsky notes, "When a great thinker despises men, it is their laziness they despise." And this explains well Tolstoy's conflict with the Orthodox church. Despite his emphasis on Christ, personal existential connection to the divine and deep piety, Tolstoy's hyper-individualistic and lofty philosophy meant there was a disconnect between him and the church intellectuals, who could not fully understand him. They naturally saw his vulgar explorations of the depravity of humanity as an endorsement of immorality, and his criticism of the faults of the church as some kind of Atheism. Their laziness and inability to understand the magnitude of Tolstoy's labyrinthine system of thought led to Tolstoy scorn the church. A similar pattern happened with Kant that you can see in his 1798 The Dispute of the Faculties, where he responds to the attacks by Theologians on his work, who could simply not wrap their heads around his enormous body of work. Hegel, likewise defended his philosophy from the church in his Vorlesungen über die

Philosophie der Religion, again bemoaning the laziness and unearned pride of Theologians who did not take the time to understand his dialectics.

Tolstoy's specific objections about church dogmas containing untruths are already answered by Apophatic theology, which has been taught by the dogmatic mystical tradition in Orthodoxy for 2,000 years- even in pre-Christian times with the Platonics. But Tolstoy also directly attacked some of the Church's doctrines beyond their inadequate cataphatic nature, influenced by the pietistic Lutheran movement. This unmoored quasi-Unitarianism understandably got him excommunicated, but beyond the specific disputes, there was also a broader disconnect caused by the sheer complexity of his philosophical system and his vast body of literature, which often strayed into dark themes. In particular, his novel The Resurrection was used at the Holy Synod of February 1901 as evidence that he denied the Trinity and the divinity of Christ. He did not fight this excommunication - for his individualised piety, adopted from the Protestant-turned-atheist Continental philosophers, had led him to deny many dogmas. But he retained great admiration for some of the deep piety and intellectualism of the Russian Church, and spent his life meditating on the deep workings of God in the world and the nature of the divine law that applies to all. Dostoevsky was more grounded, but both metaphysicians asked the same questions about what it means to be authentically human. Tolstoy's lifelong, unyielding devotion to truth, his passionate recognition of the Imago Dei in all those he encountered, his costly defense of the poor and oppressed, and his violent struggle against his darker side are, ironically, awfully Eastern Orthodox of him.

Do Not Lie: Solzhenitsyn's Echo of Tolstoy's Piety

Let your credo be this: Let the lie come into the world, let it even triumph even. But not through me.

Khrushchev hailed Solzhenitsyn as "our contemporary

Tolstoy", ironically coming from the leader of the former Communist Party that had banned Tolstoy's books and banned Solzhenitsyn as well. Khrushchev used Solzhenitsyn to document Stalin's crimes, especially the gulags, which he abolished and allowed over 1 million prisoners to return home, thus correcting a lie that his predecessor had dogmatized. There is a huge overlap between these two great writers, as Solzhenitsyn builds on Tolstoy, Gogol and Dostoyevsky. There were also significant differences in their philosophy, but a single line rings true between Solzhenitsyn and Tolstoy - do not lie.

In the novel Cancer Ward, Solzhenitsyn describes the great enemies of the Marxist religion as the false socialist, the foreign capitalist, the traitor to the great cause, the unevolved man, the theist and the individualist. This problem of collectivist movements erasing the individual as the fundamental and most important unit of society is a problem on which Tolstoy commented extensively. Cancer Ward is written with a melancholy and sombre brilliance, with costly humour and a subtle, gentle return to neo-Tolstoyevskian piety. Here we see philosophical notes told through intimate psychological portraits that would snowball a decade later through The First Circle, Lenin in Zurich, and The Gulag Archipelago; humble charcoal sketches that would challenge an empire.

Solzhenitsyn notes that Lenin argued that we must 'resist the evil' of Tolstoy because he denied the Marxist axiom that men live by the 'interests of society'. Tolstoy's meditations on death were existential in nature, which naturally usurps collectivist tendencies. His answer that "people live by love" and that love is by definition irrational (or rather supra-rational) contradicts the progressive dialectic. This was seen as anti-humanist and contrary to the official Marxist philosophy of the state. Tolstoy, along with Dostoevsky, was on the long list of books banned by the USSR for promoting ideas that contradicted the revolution. Solzhenitsyn quietly points this out throughout the narrative, but ironically The Cancer Ward was immediately censored in Russia. It was added to the pile of 'evidence' that eventually led to his exile. The character of Nikolayevich is happy to accept the state teachings - he sees a future for himself in the post-Stalin USSR, and his lymphoma is on the retreat. Yefrem quietly disagrees; his time is short, and his little blue Tolstoy book has made him think seriously for the first time in his life about death, and subsequently about what is 'evil', not to the collective in which he has lived all his life - but to the individual soul.

One clear element in Solzhenitsyn that places him in the company of the great Russian writers of the 20th century is his insistence on his own participation in the evils of his society. His characters, even his protagonists, are not morally good. Rather, what makes Oleg a protagonist is his willingness to admit the evil he is capable of committing and to respond by trying to transcend his environment and move towards the objective good, i.e. holiness. This trait is present in Tolstoy's literature, but reached its apotheosis in Dostoyevsky. Dostoevsky's most depraved, nihilistic and malevolent characters are also the protagonists - almost never the antagonists of the story.

Being, not Environment, determines Consciousness: Tolstoyevskian Wisdom in the face of Socialism

Because of his focus on communal living and equality of all people, Tolstoy's words were used by various Communist writers to justify great horrors, so he cannot be seen as a prophet as we can call Dostoevsky, who warned and predicted the genocides of Stalin perfectly. As Camus noted, "the real prophet of the 20th century was not Marx, but Dostoevsky". Lenin believed that Tolstoy's call for peaceful change in Russian society helped move the revolution forward, but his Pacifism, absolute moral code and non-resistance prevented the Proletarian from rising to power. Tolstoy certainly strayed into reactionism at points and gave room for dangerous metapolitics, but as much depravity as there is in his most irreverent works, there is greater redemption in his most pious. He advocated for unity and brotherhood at an individual level, not a top-down government system and would have hated the hubris and inverted compassion of the Soviets.

Solzhenitsyn agreed with Dostoevsky that Tolstoy's works are so lofty and oceanic that they cannot be applied. Tolstoy condemned Socialism as a new dictatorship of the Proletariat, writing that "So far the capitalists have ruled, then worker functionaries would rule." But at the same time, he was blamed by some for having inspired the 1905 revolution. Solzhenitsyn's character muses on Tolstoy's influence:

'You mean Christian socialism, is that right?' asked Oleg, trying to guess. It's going too far to call it "Christian". There are political parties that call themselves Christian Socialists in societies that emerged from under Hitler and Mussolini, but I can't imagine with what kind of people they undertook to build this kind of socialism. At the end of the last century, Tolstoy decided to spread practical Christianity through society, but his ideas turned out to be impossible for his contemporaries to live with, his preaching had no link with reality. I should say that for Russia in particular, with our repentances, confessions, and revolts, our Dostoevsky, Tolstoy, and Kropotkin, there's only one true socialism, and that's ethical socialism. That is something completely realistic.'
Kostoglotov turned up his eyes.

Solzhenitsyn lived the horrors that Tolstoy was afraid of. Solz emphasizes the folly of both the naive Tsarists and the blind Reactionaries. The Tsarist regime squandered deep patriotism through bureaucratic incompetence: "Those who obtain promotion easily never seriously considered that the art of war changes every decade and that it is their duty to keep learning, adjust to new developments, and keep abreast of the times." Dostoevsky had this same argument with Gogol, who was a Tsarist. While they shared a detest of the revolutionaries, Dost warned Gogol of absolving it of all wrongdoing. Solzhenitsyn has this same view- the Tsarist regime was its own worst enemy and created the revolutionaries through its insipid arrogance, pride, and wilful ignorance. Dost in the late 19th century, and Solzhenitsyn in the late 20th century both eventually came to the same political position of advocating for a self-aware and self-critical patriotism, while condemning Nationalism and its antipodal reactionism. This paradoxical dynamic was put on display in the fact that the assassin of Pyotr Stolypin (Prime Minister of Russia 1906-1911) worked for both the Tsarist secret police and the Arachno-Communist Revolutionaries at the same time.

Entering WWI was one of these Tsarist follies that helped create the Revolution: "It would have, of course, been much jollier to stand side by side with Germany in an eternal alliance as Dostoevsky had so fervently wished and advised." Vanya, the starry-eyed Tolstoyevskian, meets his hero but is inevitably drawn into a war he does not belong in. To many at this time, Tolstoy was a unifying philosophy that sits above the chaotic religious and political environments stemming from the introduction of central European forms of Protestantism (Anabaptism, Neo-Arian Jehovah's Witnesses etc) and various Socio-Economic ideologies. The 'devil' that possessed Solz was Marx's toxic mixture of the English social empiricism of Hume, Locke, and Smith with the Hegelian dialectic of progressive history infused French Utopianism. This philosophic parasite, a Frankenstein creation of the worst bits of Continental and Analytic Philosophy, eradicated the historic Russian ethos. It brushed aside the wisdom of Tolstoy and Dostoevsky and became 'possessed' by the devils of Epicurean Socio-Political religions, crushing the vessels it inhabited:

However wary you are, in seven long years the abominable tranquility of an essentially petit-bourgeois existence will lull your vigilance. In the shadow of something big, you lean against a massive iron wall without looking at it carefully- and suddenly it moves, it runs out to be a big red engine wheel driven by a long, naked piston rod, your spine is twisted and you are down! you belatedly realize that yet again some stupid danger has taken you unawares.

In Aleksandr Solzhenitsyn's The First Circle, his character Volodin muses about Epicureanism's influence on Marxism, something Tolstoy warned of in his article On Socialism and his "Letter to the Liberals":

> The highest criteria of good and evil are our own feelings of pleasure or displeasure' In other words, according to Epicurus, only what I like is good and what I do not like is evil. This was the philosophy of a savage. Because Stalin liked killing people did this mean that he regarded killing as good? And if someone found displeasure in being imprisoned for having tried to save another man, was his action therefore evil? No – for Innokenty good and evil were now absolute and distinct, and visibly separated by the pale-grey door in front of him, by those whitewashed walls, by the experience of his first night in prison. Seen from the pinnacle of struggle and pain to which he was now ascending, the wisdom of Epicurus seemed no more than the babbling of a child.

Remember your Death and you will not Sin

Solzhenitsyn directly mimicked Tolstoy's 1886 The Death of Ivan Ilyich (Смертъ Ивана Ильича) with his 1962 "One Day in the Life of Ivan Denisovich". The Russian Greats repeatedly focused on the certainty of biological death as the penultimate fact, the only fact of life that is true, absolute, or relevant. In A confession, Tolstoy extrapolates this idea which Ivanovic faces in the story: "No matter how often I may be told, 'You cannot understand the meaning of life so do not think about it, but live,' I can no longer do it: I have already done it too long. I cannot now help seeing day and night going round and bringing me to death. That is all I see, for that alone is true. All else is false."

Tolstoy's sketch of the life of Pyotr Ivanovic represents a critical nexus in his thinking following his 1870's conversion around the linchpin of the "only true fact" of death. This is his aetiological exploration of what the ramifications of knowing one's own death experientially; a pensive, autobiographical and metaphysical musing on what it means to truly live a life with meaning; here he draws a difference between a societal understanding of goodness and 'true life', i.e., maintaining a metaphysical relationship with Goodness. In pure Tolstoyan form, The Death of Ivan Ilyich is designed to make you uncomfortable.

This line of thinking was adopted but taken in a very different direction by Nietzsche, Camus, and their secularist disciples. Tolstoy's Epistemology is subtly different from Camus' and it leads to fundamentally different conclusions about the meaning of life. Tolstoy sees this unavoidable reality of death as illuminating super-realities; Camus does not. Tolstoy sees the fact of death as a truism that demands a relationship with the eternal and a reason to feel deeper and live better; Camus, in his craven narcissism, sees this reality as an anodyne. Tolstoy sees it as morally transformative; Camus sees it as morally disintegrating. Camus takes this immutable fact one-dimensionally, and in the abyss of French materialism, sees no metaphysical principle to extrapolate from it.

Tolstoy muses that an openly evil life is not as wrong as a comfortable and happy life, displaying how much he hated Epicureanism: "Ivan lived a life most simple and most ordinary and therefore most terrible." In other words, Ivanovic's choice to make happiness the penultimate goal on a day-by-day basis was the choice to embrace absolute death. And here near his end, he found no community to ease his pain. "And he has to live like this, alone, on the edge of destruction, with nobody at all to understand and to pity him. There has been daylight; now, there is darkness. I have been here; now, I am going there. Where? He could hear nothing except the beating of his own heart." This is intensely autobiographical, for Tolstoy was quite irreverent and pushed everyone away from him before his religious conversion. In his old age, he became more pious and reconciled with his wife, whom he had mistreated.

Tolstoy's story ends simultaneously hopeful and bitter. In his last hours, he finally repents and releases the hate and arrogance and embraces the divine, but his family never understood this. Death was no more for Ivanovic, not because he was not going to die, but that final development in his moral fortitude towards a silent but real repentance brought him life for the first time. In Tolstoy's post-conversion life, he began to sketch the reality that living a 'good' life where you assert your goodness and right to heave up on never having done anything horrible is not enough to be genuinely alive; an active relationship with goodness through repentance and self-denial is necessary; all else is a living death. At his end, Ivanovic found his beginning.

The omnipotent narrator of Cancer Ward notes "the whole of his life had prepared Pudduyev for living, not for dying". In the chapter titled "Idols in the marketplace", the patients argue about death and whether one should acknowledge it. Some do not want to, because the recognition- the awareness and understanding of the implications of the end of life- is contrary to the Socio-political 'Idols of the tribe' which they have lived their life in service to. Personal acceptance of their own pending non-existence threatened their Marxist ideology, and thus their emotional homeostasis, and the very purpose of their life in the first place. Dostoevsky used the metaphor of Demons; Solzhenitsyn uses the imagery of Idols.

> Because what do we keep telling a man all of his life? 'You're a member of the collective!' You're a member of the collective!' That's right. But only when he's alive. He may be a member, but he has to die alone.

Decades later, Solzhenitsyn finishes this thought in his 1978 Harvard Commencement speech:

> If humanism were right in declaring that man is born only to be happy, he would not be born to die. Since his body is doomed to die, his task on earth evidently must be of a more spiritual nature. It cannot be unrestrained enjoyment of everyday life. It cannot be the search for the best ways to obtain material goods and then cheerfully get the most of them. It has to be the fulfilment of a permanent, earnest duty so that one's life journey may become an experience of moral growth, so that one may leave life a better

human being than one started it.

Tolstoy may have not been a Saint, but he died a Stoic. Appended to his 1884 Confessions are his last notes written on his deathbed, where he expresses his last his last doubts and his last hopes:

I cannot even make out whether I can see anything down there, in that bottomless abyss over which I am hanging and to which I am being pulled. My heart clenches, and I feel horror. ... The infinity below repels and horrifies me; the infinity above attracts and affirms me. In the same way I am hanging on the last of my last, not yet sprung out from under me, over the abyss; I know that I am hanging, but I look only upward, and my fear passes away. As it happens in a dream, some voice says: "Notice this, this is it!"... All this was clear to me, and I was happy and calm. And it was as if someone was saying to me: look, remember.

And I woke up.

Tim Newcomb
Stuttgart, Germany
Summer 2023

Tolstoy's Life and Works

1828: Birth of Leo Tolstoy

Leo Tolstoy is born on September 9th in Yasnaya Polyana, Russia, into a noble and wealthy family.

1830-1839: Early Education and Family Life

Tolstoy begins his education in Kazan, Russia, and later moves to Moscow. His mother passes away when he is just nine years old.

1844-1851: University Studies and Military Service

Tolstoy enrolls in the University of Kazan to study law but leaves without completing his degree. He then joins the Russian army and serves in the Crimean War.

1852-1857: Travel and Writing

Tolstoy embarks on extensive travels throughout Europe, which profoundly influences his worldview. During this period, he writes his first major works, the trilogy "Childhood", "Boyhood" And "Youth".

1859: Charles Darwin publishes "On the Origin of Species"

Darwin's groundbreaking work introduces the theory of evolution, challenging traditional religious beliefs and shaping intellectual discourse. Nietzsche and other intellectuals begin parsing out the ramifications.

1862-1869: Marriage and "War and Peace"

Tolstoy marries Sophia Behrs and begins work on his epic novel "War and Peace." The novel, published in installments, explores the complexities of Russian society during the Napoleonic era including the brutality of war and the fragility of life.

1867: Karl Marx publishes "Das Kapital"

Marx's seminal work in socialist theory analyzes capitalism

and examines the dynamics of class struggle.

1875-1877: "Anna Karenina"
Tolstoy completes and publishes his masterpiece "Anna Karenina," a novel that delves into themes of love, adultery, and societal expectations.

1879: Friedrich Nietzsche publishes "Thus Spoke Zarathustra"
Nietzsche's work presents ideas on the Übermensch and the death of God, challenging conventional moral and religious beliefs and advocating for full anarchism.

1886-1889: "The Death of Ivan Ilyich" and Family Conflicts
Tolstoy publishes the novella "The Death of Ivan Ilyich," which examines mortality and the search for meaning in life. He also faces conflicts with his wife and family due to his radical beliefs and rejection of wealth.

1901: "Resurrection" and Social Activism
Tolstoy releases his final novel, "Resurrection," focusing on themes of redemption and social injustice. This is the novel which finally begins his Excommunication, because it denied and questioned may doctrines and exhibited a form of Universalism. He becomes increasingly involved in social activism, advocating for nonviolent resistance and communal living but a rejection of Socialism, which he saw as worse than any type of Capitalism.

1905: Albert Einstein publishes the theory of special relativity
Einstein's revolutionary scientific theory challenges established notions of space, time, and the nature of reality. Einstein's friend Jung begins exploring the psychological ramifications of Quantum Mechanics.

1908-1910: Excommunication and Later Works

The Russian Orthodox Church excommunicates Tolstoy for his radical and ambiguous views on sexual morality, condemnation of some of the sacraments of the church, and radical socio-economic positions. Only 7 years later would the church's decision be justified as Lenin takes power and the Holodomor genocide begins in the name of the communist precepts Tolstoy endorsed. He continues writing and publishing works like "The Kreutzer Sonata" and "The Living Corpse."

1910: Death of Leo Tolstoy

Leo Tolstoy dies on November 20th at Astapovo railway station, after leaving his home in Yasnaya Polyana in search of a simple, ascetic life. His legacy as a writer and philosopher continues to influence generations.

1917: The Russian Revolution

The Russian Revolution leads to the fall of the Russian monarchy and the establishment of a communist government under Vladimir Lenin, marking the beginning of decades of genocide and authoritarianism in the name of Equity

Glossary of Philosophic Terminology in Tolstoy

Soul (Душа/Dusha)

The immaterial essence component of an individual, representing their true inner self and moral nature. Tolstoy emphasized the significance of the soul as the core of human identity and the source of moral values. Tolstoy always maintains a Platonic Numinal divide between Soul and the material world, as did Schopenhauer between Will and body.

"The sole meaning of life is to serve humanity."

Truth (Истина/Istina)

The objective reality or knowledge that accurately reflects the nature of the world and human existence. Tolstoy viewed truth as a fundamental pillar of life, guiding individuals towards genuine understanding and moral action, and oscillated on the source or origin of truth.

"Truth, like gold, is to be obtained not by its growth, but by washing away from it all that is not gold."

Goodness (Добро/Dobro)

The moral quality of actions or intentions that are beneficial, virtuous, and in accordance with higher values. Tolstoy emphasized the importance of goodness as a guiding principle for human conduct and the foundation for a harmonious society.

"The highest happiness is when one reaches the summit of their own being, and they are good to others."

Evil (Зло/Zlo)

The presence of harmful or morally corrupt actions, intentions, or qualities that oppose goodness and truth. Tolstoy acknowledged the existence of evil in the world and highlighted the moral struggle between good and evil in human affairs.

"All the variety, all the charm, all the beauty of life is made up of light and shadow."

Morality (Нравственность/Nravstvennost')

The principles and values that govern right and wrong conduct, guiding individuals towards ethical behavior. Tolstoy explored moral questions and emphasized the importance of living a morally upright life based on universal principles, in opposition to Hume and the English Empiricists.

"The law of love could be best understood and learned through little children."

Will (Воля/Volya)

The faculty or power of making choices and decisions, often influenced by desires, reason, or external factors. Tolstoy recognized the significance of individual will in shaping one's destiny and determining the course of actions.

"Man cannot possess anything as long as he fears death. But to him who does not fear it, everything belongs."

God (Бог/Bog)

Tolstoy never denied the divine, and argued against the flat rational Atheism of the Continentals and English Utilitarians. Tolstoy grappled with theological questions and examined the role of faith and spirituality in human life.

"God sees the truth, but waits."

Religion (Религия/Religiya)

A system of beliefs, practices, and values concerning the spiritual and transcendent aspects of human existence. Tolstoy critically analyzed organized religion and emphasized the importance of personal religious experience and direct connection with God.

"Religion is one of the forms of spiritual oppression, not necessarily limited to religion."

Freedom (Свобода/Svoboda)

The state of being unrestricted or liberated from external constraints, allowing individuals to act and think independently. Tolstoy advocated for personal freedom and challenged social and political structures that impeded individual autonomy.

"True life is lived when tiny changes occur."

Reason (Разум/Razum)

The capacity for logical thinking, rationality, and intellectual understanding, enabling critical analysis and comprehension. Tolstoy valued reason as a tool for seeking truth, resolving conflicts, and making informed decisions.

"The strongest of all warriors are these two: Time and Patience."

Moral Awakening (Нравственное пробуждение/Nravstvennoe probuzhdenie)

The process of becoming aware of and recognizing one's moral responsibilities, leading to personal growth and transformation. Tolstoy explored the concept of moral awakening as a catalyst for individuals to reassess their values and strive for moral improvement.

"Everyone thinks of changing the world, but no one thinks of changing himself."

Острота (Ostrota)

The sharpness or intensity of perception, often associated with a heightened sensitivity to the beauty and depth of the world. Tolstoy appreciated the concept of "острота" as a way to describe a heightened awareness of life's intricacies.

"The strongest of all warriors are these two: Time and Patience."

Тоска (Toska)

A deep longing or melancholic yearning, often associated with an intense spiritual or existential longing for meaning and connection. Tolstoy explored the concept of "тоска" as a powerful human emotion that can drive individuals to seek profound truths.

"All happy families are alike; each unhappy family is unhappy in its own way."

Смирение (Smirenie)

Humility or meekness, often understood as a virtue encompassing modesty, selflessness, and the absence of pride or arrogance. Tolstoy regarded "смирение" as an essential quality for individuals seeking moral and spiritual growth.

"In the name of God, stop a moment, cease your work, look around you."

Духовное пробуждение (Dukhovnoe probuzhdenie)

Spiritual awakening, referring to a transformative process of expanding consciousness and deepening one's connection to the divine or higher truths. Tolstoy contemplated the concept of "духовное пробуждение" as a means to transcend the material world and discover profound spiritual insights.

"Everyone thinks of changing the world, but no one thinks of changing himself."

Самопознание (Samopoznanie)

Self-awareness or self-knowledge, involving a deep understanding and introspection of one's own thoughts, emotions, and values. Tolstoy emphasized the importance of "самопознание" as a pathway to personal growth and moral development.

"To get rid of an enemy one must love him. Love him and forgive him."

Благодать (Blagodat')

Grace, often referring to the unmerited and divine favor bestowed upon individuals, leading to spiritual enlightenment or salvation. Tolstoy explored the concept of "благодать" as a transformative force that can inspire individuals towards moral and ethical living.

"The only absolute knowledge attainable by man is that life is meaningless."

Вечность (Vechnost')

Eternity, representing a timeless and infinite state beyond the constraints of temporal existence. Tolstoy contemplated the concept of "вечность" as a way to understand the transcendent nature of human life and the pursuit of higher truths.

"If there is no immortality of the soul, then there is no virtue, and there is no moral law."

Интуиция (Intuitsiya)

Intuition, referring to the ability to grasp truths or insights without relying on conscious reasoning or logical analysis. Tolstoy recognized the power of "интуиция" as a source of knowledge that can provide deeper understanding of life's mysteries.

"The two most powerful warriors are patience and time."

Сопротивление (Soprotivlenie)

Resistance or nonviolent resistance, denoting the act of opposing or challenging oppressive systems or unjust actions through peaceful means. Tolstoy advocated for "сопротивление" as a moral and effective method for social and political change.

"Wrong does not cease to be wrong because the majority share in it."

Сверхразум (Sverkhrazum)

Superconsciousness or higher consciousness, representing an expanded state of awareness beyond ordinary perception. Tolstoy explored the concept of "сверхразум" as a means to access deeper insights and connect with universal truths.

"The sole meaning of life is to serve humanity."

Соборность (Sobornost)

Communion or spiritual unity, referring to a harmonious and interconnected state of being where individuals transcend their individual selves and unite as a collective whole. Tolstoy embraced the idea of "соборность" as a way to foster empathy, compassion, and cooperation among people.

"All, everything that I understand, I understand only because I love."

Внутренняя свобода (Vnutrennyaya svoboda)

Inner freedom, denoting a state of liberation from internal constraints, such as fears, desires, and attachments. Tolstoy emphasized the importance of cultivating "внутренняя свобода" as a way to achieve authentic selfhood and live in accordance with one's true moral values.

"True life is lived when tiny changes occur."

Патриотизм (Patriotizm)

Patriotism, referring to a strong sense of loyalty, love, and devotion towards one's country or nation. Tolstoy explored the concept of "патриотизм" and questioned its implications, examining the moral responsibilities of individuals towards their nation and humanity as a whole.

"Patriotism in its simplest, clearest, and most indubitable meaning is nothing

but an instrument for the attainment of the government's ambitious and mercenary aims."

Христианская любовь (Khristianskaya lyubov')
Christian love, representing the unconditional and selfless love espoused by the teachings of Christianity. Tolstoy emphasized the transformative power of "христианская любовь" as a moral imperative and a way to foster harmony and compassion in society.

"Love is life. All, everything that I understand, I understand only because I love."

Исповедание (Ispovedanie)
Confession or self-examination, involving a sincere and introspective examination of one's thoughts, actions, and moral shortcomings. Tolstoy valued the practice of "исповедание" as a means of personal growth, moral reflection, and striving towards a higher ethical standard.

"In the name of God, stop a moment, cease your work, look around you."

Made in the USA
Monee, IL
18 November 2024